PINOCCHIO

Louis Weber, C.E.O.
Publications International, Ltd.
7373 North Cicero Avenue
Lincolnwood, Illinois 60646

Manufactured in U.S.A.

8 7 6 5 4 3 2 1

ISBN: 0–7853–1025–8

Cover Illustration by Tim Huhn

Illustrations by Gary Torrisi

Contributing Writer: Dorothea Goldenberg

PUBLICATIONS INTERNATIONAL, LTD.

Long ago a poor old craftsman named Geppetto spent his days creating splendid wooden dolls and puppets. Geppetto's greatest joy—besides his dog, Trooper—was the shining eyes and excited laughter of the children who played with his toys. He was happy with work and happy with life, but he did have one secret wish: that someday he would be a father to a real boy.

The blue-winged fairy wanted to reward Geppetto for his good heart. She waved her magic wand as he carved a figure from a piece of fresh, soft pine wood. The little puppet seemed to come alive and giggle and wiggle in his hands.

"You are the finest puppet I have ever made," said Geppetto when he finished. "I will call you Pinocchio! Now hold still so I can paint you, you rascal."

As soon as the old carver finished, Pinocchio jumped up and scampered around the room. Eager to see the whole world, the careless little puppet ran out the door and to the village square. Such a wonderful place! It was full of shops, vendors, fruit, bread, sausages, and more. He darted through the crowd looking at every stall and in every window.

Geppetto and Trooper ran after Pinocchio because they thought he might get into mischief. And, of course, he did! Looking up and not ahead, Pinocchio did not see the cart piled high with cheeses. With a bump and a crash, the cheese cart toppled over.

Pinocchio ran, and the town policeman ran after him. The policeman grabbed Pinocchio tightly saying, "This one should be in school, not into the cheeses."

Geppetto knew that Pinocchio should be in school. The old carver sold his only coat to buy Pinocchio a school book. He gave it to him, saying, "Pinocchio, to be like a real boy you must go to school. Now on your way, and take Trooper with you. He'll help to guide you."

Pinocchio started off to school with Trooper following close behind. At the corner, Pinocchio heard the music of the local puppet show and stopped to watch it. Now Trooper knew that Pinocchio shouldn't stay, so he began to growl and tug at the puppet's sleeve. "Trooper, leave me be. I want to watch." But Trooper just growled louder.

All the noise interrupted the show, and Mr. Grumbolo, the puppet master, became very angry. He shouted at Pinocchio and Trooper, and chased them away.

Pinocchio and Trooper went on their way. At the next turn, they met Sly Fox. When the fox heard that Pinocchio was on his way to school, he shook his head and laughed.

"Oh no, no, my friend! That is not for you. Real boys don't want school. They want to sail across the Truant Sea to Runaway Island where they have fun and play all day. I could sell you a ticket if you like."

Trooper didn't care for this Sly Fox or his ideas, and he growled loudly. But some puppets just won't listen. Quicker than a wink, Pinocchio traded his school book for a ticket to Runaway Island. He was going to be a real boy and have fun.

As Sly Fox ran off, the blue-winged fairy appeared. "Pinocchio, why aren't you going to school?" she asked.

"Oh, but I am! I was just... I was just helping that fellow find his way to town." And with that big lie, Pinocchio's nose began to grow longer and longer until a butterfly flew down and sat on it.

Pinocchio began to cry. He promised to be a good boy and go straight to school. The fairy forgave him and with a sweep of her wand, he got his old nose back.

When Pinocchio got to school, he met Wickley, a boy who was leaving for Runaway Island. Pinocchio forgot all about Geppetto and the fairy. He would not listen to Trooper. He just went along to Runaway Island.

At first Runaway Island seemed wonderful. It was all carnivals, sweets, and bicycles, and no one telling you what to do. Pinocchio and Wickley played all day. Trooper stuck close by but would have nothing to do with the fun.

They stopped by a lake to rest, and as Pinocchio dipped his hand into the water for a drink, he saw his reflection. Yikes! He had grown long ears and a tail like a donkey. He turned to Wickley and saw that it was happening to him, too, and to all the other boys on the island. Pinocchio cried out, "Oh, help . . . somebody please help me!"

Once again, the blue-winged fairy appeared. "Foolish puppet," she said, "lose those donkey ways and go find your poor father who cries for you."

With a wave of her wand, the fairy took away the donkey ears and tail, and sent Pinocchio down to the seashore. He could see Geppetto far out to sea in a small boat. Like any father would, he was searching tirelessly for his lost son.

As Pinocchio called out to him, the water began to churn and foam terribly. From the depths of the sea a huge wave rolled up, and on that wave rode a giant fish. The fish swallowed up Geppetto, boat and all.

Thinking only of his father, Pinocchio dove in the water, swam out to the fish, and jumped right down its throat without even blinking.

Deep in the belly of the fish, Pinocchio and Geppetto hugged each other and danced with joy. They were so happy to be together. But how to get out?

Geppetto thought and thought, but he could not come up with a plan. As they sat and schemed, they heard an enormous rumbling noise that seemed to come from everywhere. "Snoring!" cried Pinocchio. "The fish is asleep! Come on, Father, when he opens his mouth to snore, we'll slide down his tongue and slip out between his teeth."

The plan could not have worked better. In a moment, the two were free again.

But they were still far from shore. Geppetto's boat was gone, and the old puppet maker was not a good swimmer. Coughing and spluttering, he said, "I don't know if I can make it to shore!"

Pinocchio saw his father begin to sink in the waves. The little puppet grabbed him by the arm and pulled him all the way to the shore to safety.

Geppetto awoke on shore with the waves gently rushing up at his feet. Next to him sat Trooper, watchful and loyal. And in front of him sat, of all things, a little boy! Not a puppet, not a doll, but a real live boy named Pinocchio! Geppetto lifted the boy up in his arms.

"Pinocchio, what happened to you?" Geppetto exclaimed.

"The blue-winged fairy was here," answered the little boy. "She turned me into a real boy. She said that I had finally learned that being a real person simply means caring about others."